claim

& other stories

ALSO BY KRIS HAGGBLOM

Ghosts of Beautiful Women Dancing
Light Trace Glass Trap
Crossing Paradise
Inside the Wires
Dream Without a Dreamer
Consolation Prize
Chain of Silence
The Book Thief
Broken Time Machine
Exposure
Glints (a chapbook series)*
Solar Microscope
Solidago Wars
Twenty Flowers in the Ancient Manor
Features of Our Hacked Lagoon
Have You Preyed Today?
Seven Dragonflies I & II
No Song
Dawn of the New Age
Ghosts in the Wind
The Black Rose
CamerAcker

claim
& other stories

Kris Haggblom

POETIC JUSTICE BOOKS
PORT ST. LUCIE, FLORIDA

Published by Poetic Justice Books
Port Saint Lucie, Florida

ISBN: 978-1-950433-69-8

FIRST EDITION
10 9 8 7 6 5 4 3 2 1

contents

claim
& other stories

the book thief

A book thief lives in my building. I know he lives there because I have seen him go in and come out many times and on more than one occasion we have exchanged greetings.

– Hello.

– Good afternoon.

One Thursday evening, he arrived at the building's outside door at the same time as I. He was carrying two large boxes that seemed to weigh heavily upon him.

– Hi.

– Good evening.

There was no sign of strain in his voice, but he was noticeably relieved when, after I had opened and held the door for him, I offered to share his burden.

– Can I give you a hand?

– Thank you, yes.

The box was quite heavy and I wondered how far he had carried the two himself. He went up first and I followed him to the second floor. He put his box down in front of the door just to the left of the stairwell. I put the other box on top of the first as he turned the key in his door.

– There you go.

– Thank you very much.

I stood there, awkwardly curious, staring at the boxes.

– They're awfully heavy, aren't they?

– Yes, that they are.

I still gazed at the boxes. Perhaps a marking of some kind…

– What's in them?

– They are additions to my collection.

– I see.

I stood watching as he bent into the first box. He straightened up with it and looked at me.

– Are you curious?

– Yes. Very.

– Can you keep a secret?

– Yes, I believe so.

He looked me over as if he were reading a chart. He checked me off as trustworthy, grinned, turned and went into his room.

– Bring in the box and close the door behind you.

I grabbed the box and kicked the door to as I passed it.

– You may put the box down anywhere. Would you like a cup of tea?

– Thank you, that would be nice.

I put the box down and peered around in the dim light. The room was full of shelves and the shelves were overflowing with books. From the floor to the ceiling – books. I had never seen so many books outside the public library or B. Dalton's.

There were no windows. They were covered by shelves. The only light came from a table lamp that was propped atop what had once been a tacky patterned sofa but was now an undefined lump with different shades of grey thrown about. He must have slept on it, because the only other piece of furniture was a fruit crate standing at the end of the lump. The crate had books in it, but only one on top.

– Come here.

I went into his kitchen. I was not surprised to find that filled with books also. They were all in neatly stacked boxes. Each box had a big 'X' drawn on its side. I suspected that all the cupboards were full.

He held an empty tin.

– I'm sorry, there is no more tea. Would you like some orange juice?

– Sure.

He opened the refrigerator. It was almost empty except for the top shelf. That was packed with what looked like very old manuscripts.

He poured two paper cups of juice.

– Shall we see what surprises we have?

– Where?

– In the boxes, of course.

He set his cup down on the crate and dragged one of the boxes we had carried in to the foot of the sofa. He opened the box very carefully, as if the books I knew it held were made of glass. He lovingly lifted the top book from the box.

– Aaaaahhh… *The Complete Works of Rimbaud*. Excellent. I have not read this in years. Very good indeed.

– Why would you buy a book you have already read?

His giggles were like more than one child playing a joke. He pulled out another book.

– Alison Treeworth's *History of the Bottle*. I must admit I have never heard of Alison Treeworth. I do hope it is better written than Richard Conwey's.

– Who is that?

– He wrote an extremely boring treatise on bottle making in America. It was some of the most atrocious drivel to ever find a printer.

– Are you in bottling?

– Bottling? Heavens no.

The next few books were by Nathaniel Hawthorne and he claimed to have read them all. He kept giggling as he emptied the box. He made two piles as he went along: one of books he'd read and one of those he had not. He paid no attention to subject matter, or even language. Only read and not read.

When he had finished emptying the boxes with a comment for each book, he had a not read pile of seventeen and a read stack of more books than I had opened in the last ten years. I felt guilty and uneasy, the leaf that quivers when there is no breeze.

– You've read all those?

– I've read every book in this room.

– *All* of them?

He titttered again. He stood up and skipped back and forth on his feet. I stared at him and the books.

– Walk around the room. Find any book you like. Open it to the first page of the text and read me the first line. I will tell you what book it is.

I jumped up and grabbed the nearest book.

– "There is no greater impediment to the advancement of knowledge than the ambiguity of words."

– *Essays on the Intellectual Powers of Man*. Thomas Reid.

He hadn't even hesitated. I thought that perhaps it was one he had recently read since it was so near the sofa. I put it back and went to a far corner of the room. I pulled down a book.

– "Well, well, well, what's it going to be then, eh?"

– Anthony Burgess. *A Clockwork Orange*.

I grabbed another.

– "Once, if my memory serves me well, my life was a banquet where every heart revealed itself, where every wine flowed."

– *A Season in Hell* by Rimbaud. I'm so glad I've received another. You may borrow that one if you like.

I stared at him. I looked at all the shelves and boxes and stared some more. Finally, I put the book in my coat pocket.

– Would you mind terribly if I asked you to leave? I have a lot of reading to do.

– But… how can you read so…?

– Yes, quite a bit.

I went downstairs to my room. The book sat heavily in my pocket. I was not tired, so I pulled it out and found not one, but two books. I've read both but returned only Rimbaud. *A Clockwork Orange* I keep as a reminder of guilt.

but the poets lie too much

the cemetery

I saw an old man being buried today. There were several small children gathered at the black hems of pretty young mothers. Some older women were weeping silently into handkerchiefs borrowed from the few men who stood reverently beside. I knew it was an old man because there were no teenagers. Old men demand respect at a funeral.

I don't know why I was at the cemetery. I don't know anyone buried there. Perhaps, I just needed a quiet place to think. There are plenty of quiet places, but something about the cemetery… I think it's the smell. A cemetery may be a place of death, but it smells so much of life; of earth and flowers. It always seems as if there had just been a brief thunder shower, and, if I close my eyes, I could be in a forest.

the forest

A forest. That would be the proper place to think. The center, the heart of the forest. Where it always feels like rain, and smells green, and sounds dark. The air is heavy and damp and surrounds and enters me. It is so silent that I can no longer hear my heart, only the moss growing and that is the true heart.

The heart of the forest is the only place I can go and not be an outsider. I enter the heart and become the damp moss, the green liquid air. I fit and do not have to worry about *trying* to fit. I am free.

There is no forest, so I must close my eyes. The cemetery is close, but a chance plane overhead or a person nearby prevents me from becoming the cemetery as I do the green.

Since I know no one buried there, I must have gone to think. I cannot remember exactly what I had to make a special trip to think about. It must have been the letter.

the letter

I received a letter this morning from a friend who had not written for quite a long while – over two years. The letter did not tell me what had happened during that time, nor did it tell me nothing as many letters do. The letter told me a great deal. In a quick, bothersome hand, my friend related a dream that had been troubling her.

the dream

Dear K.,

What follows is a dream. It is written as clearly and closely as I can. It has something to do with you, especially since you told me one like it before.

I am lying on a bed (not my own) with a heavy quilt beneath me. The bed has tarnished brass rails. The ceiling of the room begins to melt. I do not move though I know I can. As the ceiling drips into the room, a large, grey bird hangs motionless above the bed. I am looking at the bird (an albatross?) from beneath the waves of an ocean. I enter the cave which appears before me. The bed has sunk beneath the sand; only the four corner posts remain in sight. The cave becomes a hall in a great coral castle, though the floor remains sand. The walls glow softly pink and gold and green. I hear echoes – the sound of distant time; of the past. I turn to leave and find I do not know the way back. I take one step and something (I cannot make it out clearly; a bulky shadow, as of a crowd) stirs from the sand and starts to climb up towards what I take to be the sun shining through the waves. I turn again and begin a slow walk deeper into the castle. After what must be miles of twisting turning hallways, I pass someone going in the wrong direction. Just by chance, for it did not happen with any of the other people I've passed, which suddenly seems to be many though I did not remember any a moment ago, just by chance, this stranger's and my glances meet. This stranger is you, but only for a moment because then, I am looking at myself through your eyes. I am you and what I see is me. I realize that, as you, I can help myself understand this place, so I take my hand and lead me/you through the halls. Suddenly, we are at the end of a hall. There is nothing there, just a void, kind of like a cliff. But not, just a void. I am me again and you are gone. I know I must go on and silently step forward. I am falling, slowly at first, but gradually faster. I fall through a grey shadow; the same one that had arisen behind me before. While in the shadow, I hear voices or noises or colors – I can't explain it, it's just *there* – maybe it's just sensing everything at once. There are eyes watching me as I fall past. Suddenly, everything is dark. Black; nothing. I think I am dead. I open my eyes and find myself in the brass bed, but now there is a window at the foot of the bed. Dust curls up through the light like a million bright pairs of sunlight wings. I open the window and call your name out and listen to it echo across the sky.

I've had this dream a great many times and there has never been an answer.

Love,

Erika

erika

What was I thinking today in the cemetery? Perhaps, I was simply recalling an old friendship.

I could see her sitting there on the cold stone. Her dark face with those Mediterranean blue eyes that I never lied to. I could have told her I was the king of Serbia in exile, and she would have believed me. But, she never gave me reason to. And she's wearing a black knit sweater, bunched at the elbows, and faded jeans, and no shoes.

Erika always wore something black. She said it was for the future.

And her hair; I loved her hair. It was hard to believe that someone could have so much hair. Not that it was very long, there was just so much of it. Dark brown hair, twisting and curling everywhere. And yet, it always seemed neat, as if she had carefully placed each strand. Whenever it rained, I loved to walk right behind her to catch the smell of that hair and her skin. She smelled clean and dark, like my forest.

We would sit and talk forever about a book, a movie, ourselves and our dreams.

the problem

The dream. I remember the dream that she talked of in her letter. Mine was almost identical to hers, but our roles were reversed. It was a bit different at the beginning. In my dream the ceiling doesn't melt. My bed is carried on a wave to the entrance of the castle. The rest is identical except I always received an answer to my call at the end.

After two years, a good friend tells me she has taken my dream. Now, I find I have a problem most difficult to resolve. How do I answer her? I cannot answer her as she answered me. Her answer was a feeling that came back to me. A knowledge, a reassurance.

I cannot put a feeling into an envelope. I can only put words, and words are not enough. She could get a feeling from my words, but it may not be the feeling I intended. Still, a misunderstood answer is better than no answer.

but the poets lie too much

Perhaps, *that* is why I was thinking today. I was trying to find the most accurate words and proper phrases.

Dear Erika,

I saw an old man being buried today. I knew he was old because there were no teenagers. I was reminded of your hair and the forest. We must talk. Perhaps a drink. We could read to each other – Joyce or Nietzsche. The answer must be somewhere. "But the poets lie too much." Thus spake Zarathustra.

Love,

K.

I wonder if she will understand. It is becoming a burden to think, I want to be green.

propagation

It was all kinda stupid when you think about it. But I guess that's the whole point. And with nobody to think about anything…well, there's not even a point. A bang or a whimper. Whatever – same result.

If anybody had been listening they would have heard the rumbles. The fissures snaking their way throughout the planet like a sheet of overheated glass. While everyone was yelling about climate change and equality and whose god could beat up whom, the planet was shaking itself to smithereens. Mother earth was going to shed her skin of parasitic wannabees and start over.

Some even thought they could profit from the shit. Sinking needles to draw earth's blood and burn her sky. Gouge, spit on, tie down, penetrate, use up the only mother you ever had. For a stack of promises and wind from others doing the same.

When she'd had enough of our antics, she had to scratch. And, as I said, it started with rumbles. Way down. Low. If you'd stand still you could feel it in your feet. But no one stood still. People dismissed it as an aftershock. A mere tremor, bouncing around the tectonic plates if you believed in that sort of thing. Or a punishment from above if you didn't.

But this was no simple earthquake. No slipping and settling of mountains. Gaia set herself up for a big wet dog slop fest. When she started rolling back and forth, sloshing oceans over mountains rivers over towns, people still didn't believe it. It's the Chinese! Terrorism! Alien invasion! Rapture!

And just like that ninety-three percent were gone. With no sure ground and no respite the rest were slowly reduced to zero.

The rolls continued. Mountains crashed into valleys. Water, ice and stone shaken into a viscous slop, waves a hundred feet high smashing into each other and scouring everything on the surface into a muddy froth. As the shaking accelerated pieces began to fly off into space. Water and stone flung to Mars, the moon, Venus and beyond. A solar system infected.

Perhaps we are viruses. We have finally caused our host to sneeze.

satori on the uptown a-train

The incessant pounding was beginning to get to Alsyn again. No matter what he tried – aspirin, pressing his fingers on his temples, tightly shutting his eyes and counting (to himself, of course), even standing on the ceiling and breathing inside out – nothing could make the pounding stop. It had been going on for almost two minutes now and Alsyn knew he was just about ready to have himself committed when he thought of a grand idea.

"I'll bet no one has ever thought of this before," mused Alsyn as he began to move towards his front door.

The door to Alsyn's house was green and heavy and had a black stripe (to keep out unwanteds). At least, that is what it looked like from the inside. Alsyn could not remember what astrological house the moon was in, so he did not know what the outside of his door looked like.

"I shall find out momentarily." Alsyn brought his hand to his lips. He'd almost spoken aloud with no one to hear him. "Better watch that. Let's get on with it."

The pounding was getting louder. Alsyn opened his door and the pounding stopped.

"Ahh, peace," sighed Alsyn.

"Hello! And peace to you," cried the ant, his feelers knitting the blue air above their respective heads.

The ant's appearance quite startled Alsyn, who had not been prepared to greet anyone on his doorstep, much less a five-foot-three-and-a-half-inch ant carrying a violin case, and he took a few quick steps back. The ant, naturally interpreting Alsyn's behavior as an invitation, said "Thank you" and proceeded straightaway to the living room.

Alsyn did not want to appear rude, so he did not remark on the ant's habit of sitting upon his feet on Alsyn's newly upholstered sofa. Instead, Alsyn inquired as to what had brought the ant, whose name was Chad, to his black with a green stripe (that *invited* unwanteds) door.

"Well," said Chad as he opened his violin case, "as you can see, my Variegated Strad is nigh empty, and I was wondering if you could spare a cup of Stravinsky to get her started."

"A CUP OF STRAVINSKY?!" cried Alsyn. "That's highway robbery."

"But you have a green stripe. You invited me in, now you must give me what I need. I must get my instrument started or I shall lose my position at the conservatory." Chad was nearly in tears.

"I'll give you a cup of John Cage," offered Alsyn, quickly.

"That's no good. You should know that no one can tell if you have any Cage left or not. A gallon is worth an ounce. I need something with substance."

"Oh dear, oh dear," fussed Alsyn as he tried to think of something he could spare.

"Well?" Chad was impatient and was constantly glancing at his grandfather's watch that he had received only six minutes before.

"I can spare some Bach, but only half a cup." Alsyn thought it would be worth a try.

"No! No! No!" Chad began to rip at Alsyn's new sofa. "I want a cup. I must be at the conservatory…" He glanced at his grandfather's watch.

"No," offered Alsyn, "you're in the subway."

"I know that. Why did you tell me that?" Chad was beginning to think that Alsyn was a nut case.

"Because you said you were at the conserv…"

"Stop! Stop! I do not care. I simply must have my instrument started. There is a recital tonight for the Queen. Might you have some Strauss, perhaps?"

"Strauss? Yes…yes…I think so." Alsyn hated to part with any of the ancients, but he knew the law and the law said that a green striped door was ripe. He wished it was not so.

"I'll make do with a cup of Strauss," then to himself, Chad made a mental note, "a stroke of luck. It pays to ask high."

"I'll fetch it straightaway," said Alsyn, and he went down his floorboards to the attic where he kept the garden. He could hear the music of the garden's plants as he searched for Strauss. "Two years before I can hear this again," Alsyn thought as he shook the Strauss spores off the plant and onto the uprooted vinyl where they would sprout.

"All for the Queen, of course, cursed insect," thought Alsyn as he handed the hummingplant to Chad.

Chad crushed the Strauss between his mandibles and let the juice fill his violin. He closed the case when it was full.

"Thank you," said Chad and he left, being sure to close the door on his way out.

"Ahh, peace," sighed Alsyn and he settled down to listen to the subway rattle his floorboards.

gone or going

Since one must drink, one must die.

Wine?

Bread.

Heathen.

Idolater.

Friend.

Friend.

Where have you been?

Where?

Or when.

Ahh.

…

Above.

The sky has fallen then.

When?

Yes. Yes.

When.

Still…yes.

ghosts in the wind

We are a community of strangers
  all spirits, ghosts
Haunting each other's days
  you do not see me
  I pass through you
As transparent as water
The ripples barely register
  in the sun's eyes
  gone soon enough
Dreams, broken by daylight,
  are free to explore the world
Turned out of their beds

they wander the ways and trails

of future memory

Gather them back each night

and listen

Hear tales of daring

of wonder and shame

of beauty and sorrow

If she bends to the ground

catch her tears

before they can touch the earth

Sprinkle them over your bed

ride on the visions

cast upon your pillow

But be sure to kiss

your ghosts full on the lips

before they sleep forever

An old image with battered edges

The eyes burn in her mind

from when

From when

when

she does not know

He offers his hand

She hesitates

A tentative touch

    becomes an aggressive embrace

And Tatiana

    is choking in the dust

Her language of stars

    sweeps the earth

The moon cries

    for her sister

Tatiana draws the blanket

    across her breast

    rolls away from her lover's breath

    and sleeps

Dream ghosts at her feet

When Thunder beats the Sky

    the ghosts of the wind

    ride the tears

They bang on the roofs

   and scratch at the windows

   of the sleeping lovers

Tatiana – eyes wide –

   grasps for her lover's last breath

Her fingers just brush his

   as he slips into darkness

She is standing in a grove

Someone is crying nearby

   a small terrible sound

There is no one

   and she

   falls

     to

      her knees

map to the hanging

At what point do we say "enough?" We are all so sure that we shall never reach that point – the space where we become null. We are all Hamlet, Camus, the anonymous jumper…

This is a generation of failure. We thrive on it. Failure is what motivates us. *Loser* is a badge of honor. Reality's grip on our being is tenuous at best, and as each finger slips from its hold, we glance over our shoulder and decide that chaotic fantasy, the waking dream, isn't so bad after all.

Our status as the wrong ones gives us the freedom to smash through the roofs of each other's tunnels. We all redistribute the stream, turn an ocean through itself. Perception becomes liquid, color and shape are steam, thought dismissed as the bastard son of another universe. Our minds are reborn in the drops that spray the shore, only to immediately fall back to the sea or perhaps persist in the fog that envelops the mountains of madness.

We claim to seek a sun that will burn off the mist, pretending that we do not know the mist is ourselves. We claim to seek, but do not. The fog will not be lifted and the mountains will not be saved.

Jotting notes with a pretzel and a sweat-beaded brow. Fuck your concrete poetics. My neighbor bit me when I called her a silky bitch. Brilliant Christian whores saving themselves for a dead idea. Too late they find another use for the crucifixes that their laughing fathers forced on them. Too late to fly, too far to flee.

An army of misled nuns descends upon the city. They wade into the crowds, swinging their cunt soaked crosses, filling the streets with blood and sex. With *Hail Marys* and *Our Fathers* tools of apocalypse. Apocalypse. A pair of lips spread to scream. Faster faster ohyes yes. Screams and teeth broken for all time.

Forty-seven counts of treason, any one of which will serve as an excuse for swinging. Nothing on the map, of course. May as well enjoy yourself.

The fourteen year old daughter of the mayor, a crucifix suspended between precocious breasts, lips swollen from the butt end of the rifle used to knock out her teeth. She's done crying, but the venom planted in her eyes will wait for you forever. She'll take the full fist now. No sounds. Her hatred is your true love. You are finally home as she wipes the blood from her nose with the back of her hand and snarls; animal sounds burble through.

No notes sound so deeply. The play of shadows sliding across thighs; bending sharply. Bone white reflections in flowing mix of blood and cum.

Is it possible to let her go? She cannot read the map but she needs your love. A march of force – the war of souls. You know that she will not confuse the stars with your hands, as tender as rough hewn lumber, smooth as gold.

No passage back. You carve your name in her breast with a rusty blade, lap up the blood as she cries out – only once – and rub shoe polish through the cut.

"If you leave I will die."

As you wish, and you go.

unstill life

Once, while tripping through the woods, crisp air, frogs singing, I came to a halt before a large tree. There was nothing particularly particular about this tree – maybe a little bigger than the others around it but not pretentiously so. I just stopped there. Perhaps I was tired or maybe it was that the tree was simply directly in my path. At any rate, there I was at the base of this large tree. "What *kind* of tree?" you may ask. Hmmm. A large one. Dark bark, so probably not a pine, though I won't rule that out. Definitely not a birch. Much larger and darker than a birch, anyway. So anyways, a big tree just parked right smack in my way. What is one to do? I could have stepped around it, I guess. But I didn't. I could have sat down at its base and leaned back against its rough bark and taken a snooze. But I didn't. I didn't carve my name or chop it down or take a leisurely stroll 'round its perimeter. Didn't dig up its roots or climb its branches. Didn't collect a sample or deposit one. I simply came to a halt. I stopped before this large tree. I do not know how long I stood there. Twenty minutes, twenty seconds, twenty days. Well, probably not twenty days – I have a feeling I would remember that. At any rate, some indeterminate amount of time passed. I did not speak to the tree and I don't believe the tree spoke to me. But...there was a connection, tenuous at best, established. We regarded each other. This massive, weighty ponderous being slowly turning with the sun and a self conscious lemming. Each surely finding the other stupid and ignorant. How quick the sun, how slow the earth. And then I simply turned and walked back the way I had come, my original destination lost. And now, however much time has surely melted away, I wonder. I wonder.

chain of silence

I

there is a thief in the willows

    fog tangled in her hair

she is searching for a kill

    a target

    a mark

    a sign

I left it there a long time ago

    ages

    eons perhaps

– well before recorded history at any rate

the innocence of the waterline

    is at stake

as she comes down the river

    the leaves are still

I have slipped beneath the gray mud of the bank

afraid the sound of my heart will give me away

to set in stone is to silence

my heart is plucked from the clay

    washed in the river

the gray is removed

    the stone polished

the thief hangs my heart

on a gold chain about her neck

being heartless

    therefore blind

I drift into the stream

    washed away by repeated flooding

    heading for lowest ground

    seeking depth

in stillness all is clear

I am searching for a mark long erased

II

the losses accumulate

my circle of fear expands

I am growing harder to speak with

  share with

  be with

she hides in the crowds

  readily spied

  unapproachable

hackles up

  overly alert

I venture into the new city

none touch me

few approach

I push through the sea

leaving a wake

  swirling faces

  unheard laughter

I cannot

  I refuse

to understand the language

signs piled high

    a strange flowing script

assaulted by neon

I seek refuge in a dark doorway

a shop filled with wonderful foreign scents

a wizened old man

a woman of indeterminate age and beauty

a girl unsure of her changes

a boy too sure of his cock

– the proprietor is all of these

I am given a cobalt blue bottle with a glass stopper

    redolent of cinnamon

    of cloves

    of forest and river

the glass shimmered

    winked

    grew heavy and opaline

drawn through its crystal

a heart to be possessed

I wind my hand round the stone

drowning its light in loops of blood

fire leaps

    sears my flesh

raging blindly, I hurl the stone

    through blackness

creating suns and comets

a universe of pain and privilege

    longing for chaos

III

the silence is roaring through my head

    screaming for action

a thousand throngs of lost thoughts

march just beyond my command

I have no power here

the walls have gone

I am alone

has this prison always been so cold?

my jailer refuses to be seen

she proclaims my freedom

I have no choice

    no joy

my path has been laid

    well worn

I know it well

though I have not trod it before

there is no other way

through a valley of parasites

    I carefully glide

I shiver with the cold

    my teeth chatter

    I cannot feel my fingers or feet

a fever of doubt has shaken me

the track

    once bare

    is nearly obliterated

so many others have tramped

    and trampled here

since last I was so sure

I am not my own

behind me

    the city

    faded to dust

yet the mountains still climb

my river has changed beds with the floods

the stars are still

so the stars and the mountains

will feed on the dust of the city

drinking the flood

tearing out my soul

she is hounding my steps

    though she is my prey

I cannot recall my color or shape

IV

my heart wheels aimlessly

gravity tugs

    is disobeyed

she will not show herself

she knows my helplessness

the sand has run through

    collected in her mouth

    bones

scratches against the side of a hot October rain

she melts to the rail

    dark and white

and the scraps are blown down by the twentieth century limited

no prophet's spring of come-to-pass

has dissolved the desiccation

of a late season frost

all stays still

calm

cold

weakened and bent

yet Crick's dizzying chain will not shred

I slip between the shattered slats

graying guards

no longer vigilant in their ill-chosen position

V

Is it the sleep engines that keep me up at night?

turning slowly on their shafts

grinding slowly through their past

and present

and into time

as far as I can hear

the engines moan deeply

a nightly course

of whispered creaks and broken bones

something wakes me

is it the groans of the day?

or the singing of the stars?

where are these other worlds

promised so blithely

    by the yappers of each day

I can no more focus on their buzz

then on a beam blasted through an eye

the brush

He has cut me off. Again. Though something feels more desperate, more permanent this time. Still, I can not let him go. He needs me as much as I need him. I watch helplessly as the spark goes out in his eyes. The river is calling incessantly and the wind will only take him further into a blank no man's land. A land that only he can navigate. Only he can create.

The brush moves slowly. Circling ceaselessly above the paper. Hovering. The ink in a trance. His lips begin to tremble. Eyes dart wildly as fear rises, an acrid acid burn in his throat.

I want to scream, but feel my throat tighten. I force myself to swallow the rising bile, but still cough. My eyes are burning from the strain, but I must not close them. I cannot let her get closer. So long as I have her in my sight she cannot advance. I want to curse her, to drive her back to whatever hell she's come from, but my tongue is nowhere to be found. Her lips part in a dark grimace and my tongue rolls slowly from her lips. A taste of metal fills my mouth. She rolls her head to the side, an evil grin spreads across thin lips. This creature is hungry.

His hand dips quickly, splattering ink across the paper. The brush flying wildly. Teeth and smiles – no, not smiles. Broken visages scatter rapidly. Pile upon each other. Burying stares, broken teeth and eyes. A single face in a swirl of empty. Empty. He falls to the side, brush clattering to the floor.

Was it Raphael or Azrael that offered me the wings? No matter. They only get in the way. Offer a larger target. The speed may have helped but who has time for yet another technology? And where are they now, anyway? The quill must needs suffice. The wing wielded tight in hand. Fly! Fly now afore she pounces. Burning eyes and vile. Fly afore the blackness descends. Before she wraps smothering smothering …

A ghost can only do so much. And when he refuses, then what? I can only wait. Helpless as angels. The demons are his own.

the translator

A lone woman is gathering grain in a vast field beneath a featureless sky. The field stretches horizon to horizon. Waves rippling in the constant breeze, a wind that flutters the woman's apron and plays with the curls that have slipped past the simple cotton kerchief that ties back her hair. The short, ruffled sleeves of her heavy dress bare strong arms that gather and smoothly cut the sheaves with a sickle in her left hand. A steady rhythm underscored by the gentle rolling of the whisper of strings.

Gather. Cut.

Gather. Cut.

The music sweeps along with the rolling grain. The harvest will take ten, a hundred, a thousand years at this rate. There is no hurry. She will gather as needed and provide as necessary.

Gather. Cut.

There is the slightest rumbling. Way back at the edge of the horizon. Perhaps a storm is approaching, though still so distant as to be a rumor. The sky, no longer featureless. Clouds begin to fill in from the edges.

The woman's apron, light against the dark, heavy skirt, is worn at the edges. Stained where she wipes the dirt and sweat from her hands. The sickle continues to sweep the field.

Cut. Gather.

Her eyes, reflecting the gray of a sky as luminous as the grain, are focused on nothing. A dreaming. Bent to her task, each step a hypnotic swish of fabric, a dream of hips and breasts flowing soft beneath.

Cut. Gather. Cut. Step.

The clouds slowly build. The rumble more insistent. Just as she reaches for the next sheaf a wild horse crashes through the field, a horde of thundering cossacks close behind. A swirling storm of hooves and dust. A crash of horns and drums. She is lost from our sight amid the sea of flashing horse flesh; light, shadow and dust.

One two more horsemen and the cloud settles. The rolling strings still whisper, but the field seems slightly tarnished, smaller. The woman is untouched and unmoved. Still quarter bent and sweeping in another sheaf. The sickle arcs through the shafts of sunlight, pulling the harvest in.

Gather. Cut. Step.

Her boots of soft leather, caked in mud and dust, flecked with grain like her dress, her arms, her hair. Rhythmic steps.

Gather. Cut. Step.

Gather. Cut.

The field rolls gently soft as the music of her sickle. Yet, there are more clouds now. More rumbling. The earth itself is shaking. Timpani and wind, steam and smoke as a train, tracks hidden in the grain, bears down upon the woman. Enveloped in the smoke, she continues her harvest, unaware of the thundering apparition that flattens the stalks with the wind of its passing.

The field, shaken, nearly barren, still rocks in the whisper of strings a breeze also diminished. A calm.

Step.

The clouds are roiling above. The rumbling builds, steady now. The woman stands, wipes the back of her hand across her forehead, leaving a trace of dirt. The earth is moving all around her. Dust rising from the barren earth. A thunderous roll of drums as the earth gives way around her. To the left a monumental skyscraper thrusts skyward. To the right. Behind and in front, more edifices shoot forth amid a cacophony of drums, smoke and dust. She is engulfed in the maelstrom. A boiling storm of flying earth and fire. A crescendo of strings and the smoke seems to pull back.

The woman steps forward, through the receding darkness. She is wearing a gray suit jacket and a pleated skirt, her hair tucked beneath a felt cloche. Leather strapped heals stop neatly as she scans the sheet of paper she holds in her right hand. A sudden breeze lifts the paper away from her and blows it to the left and she laughs.

The skin of her cheeks, her throat soft and smooth against the collar. The gray sparkle of diamonds plays in her eyes and her lush lips part, inviting us drawing us in.

A sharp bang and her face stutters against the frame, machine gunning light across the audience, firing spastically through the angling sprockets. The laugh frozen, eyes in a half-broken stare.

It begins as a pinhole, slightly left of center, then quickly engulfs the entire screen. A brownish smear eating dreams. All that's left to the retina a burning blast of acrid white.

Was it supposed to end that way? Did she find the just so trail through the folds, time and crumbled stone?

There are no apologies. A few impolite coughs as the souls flee into the night, smoke and ash rising to choke the dreamers as so many starving dogs.

cradle

Alon cries out for Renée and rushes into the billowing smoke. His eyes and mouth are choked with dust and grit. As he passes into the arch he is caught by the throat. Grabbed by the fist of the wind. Slammed into the wall then hurled, ragdoll flung, into the waste. Into the night.

Alon opens his eyes to the swift tilt of the stars. He tries to stand but the heavens spin him back to the ground. The soft sliding of the sand beneath him – the hum of the spheres. He closes his eyes to time's lullaby.

More sand has filtered through the cracks around the window, half burying Alon's feet. He blinks the whiteness of the sky from his eyes. The room is dark, and he has difficulty making out the shadow watching him from a far corner, her eyes swallowing his consciousness.

He tries to turn back to the window, finds himself sitting on the floor in front of her. He tries to speak, stammers, a nonsense of … …

"Don't."

Did she actually speak? He looks down at the floor, at the tip of the shiny boot just poking out from the folds of the night sky dress. Could she crush him that easily? Would she?

The beat of the wind, its waves of sand breaking against the wall, fills the square. Echoes without meaning, the substance of the stars playing games Alon would never understand. He leans forward into the fabric that wraps Renée's legs, folds his arms around them. He is sure he is going to cry or perhaps cry out. The stinging swells in his eyes as she pushes him back to the floor. He leans back on his elbows as she sweeps over him and marches to the back window. She plants her left hand against the wall and leans her head against the pane. The beating of the air slows. Alon shivers, a cool sweat running down his arms, as he watches her motionless. A silhouette praying to a smoldering sky.

Alon wants to roll up behind her. Add his comfort to her devotions. Or maybe escape through the arch, lose himself in the swirling reds of the trackless sands. Rediscover the music she taught him to see. He begins to rise.

"Don't." She has not moved. "You are not that weak."

"But I…" He stays on the floor. The wind's rhythm has revived. The air between them darker, more substantive. Alon has difficulty pushing his words across to her. "But I haven't…"

"No. Stop. It will come."

"What will? The wind claims everything I do and yet you say I am not weak. What will come?"

The light is fading away from Renée's outline, winking out the stars in her hair. The desert howling against the arch, drinking the fountain, the very stones of the square.

Alon does not know if he is dreaming. The hot spice of whispered breath covers his lips. "There is still time." There is no weight upon him. He opens his eyes to the void of night. Feels the soft motion of the earth, the sand flowing ceaselessly beneath him. His hands touch a coolness, a weightless shadow cradling him. He can see a few stars. They are not his guides.

claim

The dogs have finally been driven away by the wind. There's not much left anyway. Bayla's arm still defiantly pointing at the sky from the sand that mercifully buried her through the night. Alon's arm has no feeling left. How long has he been leaning against the window, watching the dogs, the sand devour the tiny figure at the foot of the fountain? It may have been days.

Renée grabs his shoulder and slams him around back to the wall. Her forearm pressed against his throat. "The map is not yours to give away."

He is suddenly aware of a sharp scent of lavender and nutmeg. He can feel the full weight of her body pressing into him, but he only sees the ocean fire of her eyes.

"It's mine," he manages to croak.

The spicy scent of her breath burns into his face. "It is not yours to give away," she hisses each word. "Do you understand?"

Alon knows she is sure he won't push back. The dagger, dipped in salt, a finely figured damascus kris, plunged into her throat. Spewing diamonds across the floor, rubies across her breast. His weight full upon her, his hands finding the silk of her skin slipping, he plunges further and tears open her chest. Buries his head between her breasts, within her, inhaling her heart, her being. He drives deeper within her, claiming the world. Obliterating the world. Outrunning the wind. The ocean flames subside, a purple fog obscuring the sea. A glittering rain to cool the fire. His hair hangs limply down, dripping, as he pulls himself up. The sky is sliding past his eyes as he rolls to the floor.

Renée is standing over him, adjusting her skirt. "Do. You. Understand?"

He feebly nods and brings his hand to his neck. Looks down at his chest and legs, wet. He grins up at her. She rolls her eyes, takes a breath, and feigns a kick. He winces and she slides out the door.

She is moving across the square when he pulls himself up to the windowsill. She pauses at the fountain's edge, Bayla's hand just above the top of the piling sand. She turns to look up at the window, then reaches over and pries the child fingers apart. A glint of sun is slipped between her breasts.

savior

The restaurant was noisy. A crowd of tattered so-and-sos busily not hearing each other's complaints of the day. She suddenly reaches across the stained table and grabs my arm. "You must take me to America." And still this. Still this. "How many in your family?" "Just my mother and brother." "How old?" "He's twelve." "No. You." She stabs at the plate of earthen colors. The colors of the table. Stains. Her eyes. "Take me to America." "This is America." "You lie." "This is America." The knife barely scratches the table. She drags it back and forth in front of her. Stares down at the table. The knife is pointed at my face. I sigh. "This is America." She drops her hand to the table. Her head down. A whisper. "No." The chatter around on and on. "NO!" Fist to table. A few people turn. Turn again. "This is not a dream. This is not America." I look. A face of tight rage. Pleading eyes. "There is no dream." My voice unsteady. I look to the ceiling. Close my eyes. Breathe. Breathe. I hear an inrush of breath. Feel the table violently pushed against. Chair clatters over. "You lie." I wait for the knife. I wait. Still.

Murmuring continues. Eventually I open my eyes. She is gone. A small man looks directly at me. Cocks his head imperceptibly towards the exit. Turns back to his table of mumbles. She has gone. A server, the stains on his uniform match the table, rights the chair. Slides it neatly to its place. "Please pay the cashier." He vanishes through a non-descript side door. She has gone. One of us has. Somewhere in the ruined city. I leave the restaurant. The crowd pretends to not watch my departure. Outside, I do not look for her. Yesterday's rain returned to dust.

Ruined. Not Ruined. Desolate. I was once not a stranger here. The homes still windowless. Doors closed. Closed. Against dust. Against nothing. Stranger in the street. Dust on. Dust. She determined to prove otherwise. She nods to the border. The broken bridge. "Take me to America." The dream is the bridge. She determined to prove otherwise. Not ruined. "There is no way." Dilapidated. "They say you've been." "Lies." The dust rises from my shoes. My feet. It is true but it is broken. Despite her words. "Take me to America." We. I was not the stranger.

This absence of destiny. Perhaps. Deterioration. A dust that scratches at the eyes. The ears like lazy mosquitoes. The sky rots. The sunset spoils the day. None dare whistle in the street. "Take me to America." The blind sit in windowless houses. Transcribing clouds. Each pen poised above torn sheets. Stained torn leaves. Long dissipated speeches. Dreams. Dry ink. Cracked walks leading from bolted doors to dust. Just whistling dust. Hanging pens. Each house. Hand. A martyr to absence. A monument to an abyss.

The rains have returned. The bridge broken. She stands. Matted hair. Torn clothes. Watches. Debris crashes through the river. Scrapes the channel clean. The rain. She nods across the flood. Her arms. Legs thick to the ground. She is still barefoot. The dust turned mud oozes. I stare at the water. The rain. The knife in her hand. "Why will you not take us?" "There is nowhere to go." Brown and gray.

I look up into the gray. The rain. Eyes close. Water bangs against my face. "Is it far?" Always questions. "As far as your desire." "I can kill you." I feel cold. At my throat. She is closer this time. My eyes lower to her. "So you say." She draws the blade across my throat. A gift. A caress. "So I say." She drops the gift to the ooze. Walks out the bridge. Drops from my sight.

Grateful acknowledgment is made to the following publications, where some of this work has previously appeared, sometimes in slightly different form:

Quilt/Quill, Pig Iron, Dixon Place, SpiNDec Press, TCWaRP

the translator, *cradle*, and *claim* are excerpted from the unpublished novel *Now a Minor Still Photo*.

My sincere and heartfelt thanks to the members of the Morningside Writers' Group for invaluable feedback and support.

www.ingramcontent.com/pod-product-compliance
Lightning Source LLC
Chambersburg PA
CBHW032043180726
48284CB00008B/2734